A Tale Told by Moonlight

A Tale Told by Moonlight

Leonard Woolf

ET REMOTISSIMA PROPE

Modern Voices

Modern Voices
Published by Hesperus Press Limited
4 Rickett Street, London SW6 1RU
www.hesperuspress.com

Stories from the East first published by the Hogarth Press, 1921
Growing: An Autobiography of the Years 1904–1911 first published by the
Hogarth Press, 1961
This edition first published by Hesperus Press Limited, 2006

Designed and typeset by Fraser Muggeridge studio
Printed in Jordan by the Jordan National Press

ISBN: 1-84391-424-7
ISBN13: 978-1-84391-424-2

Contents

Foreword by Victoria Glendinning   vii

A Tale Told by Moonlight   1
Pearls and Swine   15
The Two Brahmans   37

from Growing
   The Voyage Out   49
   The Pearl Fishery   59

Notes   73

Biographical note   75

'A Tale Told by Moonlight', 'Pearls and Swine' and 'The Two Brahmans' were originally published as *Stories from the East* by the Hogarth Press in a limited edition in 1921. They are presented here along with two extracts from *Growing: An Autobiography of the Years 1904–1911* by Leonard Woolf, which details his time spent as a civil servant in Ceylon.

Foreword

Few people think of Leonard Woolf as a writer of fiction. The fame and pre-eminence of his wife Virginia eclipsed his promising early foray into stories and novels. He actually published his two novels – his masterpiece *A Village in the Jungle*, and *The Wise Virgins*, both in print today – before Virginia's first novel *The Voyage Out* appeared, its publication delayed by her serious breakdown early in their marriage.

He always wanted to write, but the need to earn his living drove him, as soon as he left Cambridge, to join the colonial civil service and spend seven years as an administrator in Ceylon. It is out of his extraordinary experiences there that the stories in this book grew. Though they were written after his return to England, he was writing all the time that he was in Ceylon, in spite of the exhausting nature of his work. He anatomised Ceylon and the world he found there in long letters to his closest friend, Lytton Strachey (who kept them), and in the official diaries he was obliged to write to submit to his superiors, which were much fuller and more graphic than the general run of official diaries. He mined these sources for his stories, as he would again for the autobiographies he wrote in his old age.

The three stories reissued here were originally published (in an edition of 300 copies) by the Hogarth Press in 1921, under the title *Stories from the East*, with a vivid jacket design by Carrington of a tiger amid palm trees. Woolf wrote 'A Tale Told by Moonlight' in the period of his courtship of and engagement to Virginia Stephen. She was his intellectual equal, he respected her, and loved her unconditionally as he always would, body and soul. She could not respond to his physical desire. When they kissed she felt, she told him, like a stone. His only complete sexual experiences hitherto had been with prostitutes. With one in particular, in Ceylon, he had known ecstasy and exaltation – complicated by feelings of degradation, because there was no mental understanding between them. In 'A Tale told by Moonlight' he dramatises the desperate dilemma of a Cambridge-educated Englishman in thrall to a lovely golden-skinned Colombo prostitute with whom he can hardly communicate at all, but onto whom he projects his fantasy, if it is a fantasy, of 'something beautiful mysterious everlasting'. Woolf, with his own marital dilemma facing him, acknowledges the tragic limitations of the sexual imperative, while according to it all its overwhelming and transforming power.

'Pearls and Swine', the equally powerful second story, is based on his experience of overseeing the great pearl fishery with its vast, stinking encampment of divers, dealers and criminals, on the barren coast of Mannar in north-west Ceylon. In the story, two white administrators break down. One of them, brash and young and new to the colony, cannot withstand the flies, the heat, the stench, the violence. The other, an old Ceylon hand, has fits of DTs during which he raves and boasts obscenely about abuses he inflicted on the natives. The implication is that neither man was any good under pressure – the first because he was ignorant and shallow, the second because he had rotted morally and 'gone under', as the phrase was out East.

A rave review of *Stories from the East*, particularly praising 'Pearls and Swine', caught the eye of a literary agent, who offered to market all and any Woolf stories to American magazines for large sums of money. The American agent to whom 'Pearls and Swine' was sent was dead impressed – but found it too shocking for an American readership. 'But holy suffering cats! How Woolf can write!' Woolf, however, refused to tone it down as suggested, and effectively froze the enthusiastic agents off.

The third story, 'The Two Brahmans', is the wry retelling of a Sinhalese folk-tale. When Woolf first returned from Ceylon, he continued to read Sinhalese, which he had learned to write and speak with reasonable fluency, in preparation for writing *The Village in the Jungle*. 'The Two Brahmans' is a spin-off of his reading. Its significance, in Woolf's mind, was the destructive, constricting legacy of the caste system that, like the British class system, forced people to deny their own natures by complying with the conventions, or risk ostracism by breaking the rules. He also read and admired Joseph Conrad, and the first two stories here are strongly Conradian both in form and in spirit. (The theme of 'A Tale Told by Moonlight' is strikingly like that of Conrad's *Almayer's Folly*, published three years later in 1924.)

Woolf adopted Conrad's device of telling stories at one remove, making them into a tale told to a group of acquaintances within a 'framing' narrative. His friend E.M. Forster, reading the drafts of 'A Tale Told by Moonlight' and 'Pearls and Swine', advised him to shorten the introduction in both cases: 'This is a real technical defect.' Woolf had put an equally heavy initial 'framing' around another story, 'The Three Jews', in the first ever publication of the Hogarth Press, *Two Stories* (1917). The second story in that booklet was Virginia's 'The Mark on the Wall', which convinced Lytton Strachey that she had genius.

Strachey never felt that his friend Woolf was cut out to write fiction; his negative opinion, plus Woolf's own recognition of his wife's gift, and his urgent need to earn money for them both, discouraged him from further experiments. He confined his talent for racy narrative and characterisation to his contributions (unpublished) to Bloomsbury's 'Memoir Club', and turned to political books, to polemical journalism and to magazine editing, though he continued to write perceptive literary pieces and book reviews all his life. In all these fields, he developed crispness, confidence and irony.

The stories by Leonard Woolf that we do have are the work of a young man, still wrestling with his materials, as with his own internal conflicts, rather than controlling and exploiting them for literary ends. This artless art is precisely what gives them an irresistible urgency and pungency.

– Victoria Glendinning, 2006

A Tale Told by Moonlight

Many people did not like Jessop. He had rather a brutal manner sometimes of telling brutal things – the truth, he called it. 'They don't like it,' he once said to me in a rare moment of confidence. 'But why the devil shouldn't they? They pretend these sorts of things, battle, murder, and sudden death, are so real – more real than white kid gloves and omnibuses and rose leaves – and yet when you give them the real thing, they curl up like school girls. It does them good, you know, does them a world of good.'

They didn't like it and they didn't altogether like him. He was a sturdy thick set man, very strong, a dark reserved man with black eyebrows which met over his nose. He had knocked about the world a good deal. He appealed to me in many ways; I liked to meet him. He had fished things up out of life, curious grim things, things which may have disgusted but which certainly fascinated as well.

The last time I saw him we were both staying with Alderton, the novelist. Mrs. Alderton was away – recruiting after annual childbirth, I think. The other guests were Pemberton, who was recruiting after his annual book of verses, and Smith, Hanson Smith, the critic.

It was a piping hot June day, and we strolled out after dinner in the cool moonlight down the great fields which lead to the river. It was very cool, very beautiful, very romantic lying there on the grass above the river bank, watching the great trees in the moonlight and the silver water slipping along so musically to the sea. We grew silent and sentimental – at least I know I did.

Two figures came slowly along the bank, a young man with his arm round a girl's waist. They passed just under where we were lying without seeing us. We heard the murmur of his words and in the shadow of the trees they stopped and we heard the sound of their kisses.

I heard Pemberton mutter:

A boy and girl if the good fates please
Making love say,
The happier they.
Come up out of the light of the moon
And let them pass as they will, too soon
With the bean flowers boon
And the black birds tune
And May and June

It loosed our tongues and we began to speak – all of us except Jessop – as men seldom speak together, of love. We were sentimental, romantic. We told stories of our first loves. We looked back with regret, with yearning to our youth and to love. We were passionate in our belief in it, love, the great passion, the real thing which had just passed us by so closely in the moonlight.

We talked like that for an hour or so, I suppose, and Jessop never opened his lips. Whenever I looked at him, he was watching the river gliding by and he was frowning. At last there was a pause; we were all silent for a minute or two and then Jessop began to speak.

'You talk as if you believed all that: it's queer, damned queer. A boy kissing a girl in the moonlight and you call it love and poetry and romance. But you know as well as I do it isn't. It's just a flicker of the body, it will be cold, dead, this time next year.'

He had stopped but nobody spoke and then he continued slowly, almost sadly: 'We're old men and middle-aged men, aren't we? We've all done that. We remember how we kissed like that in the moonlight or no light at all. It was pleasant; Lord, I'm not denying that – but some of us are married and some of us aren't. We're middle-aged – well, think of your wives, think of –' he stopped again. I looked round. The others were moving

4

uneasily. It was this kind of thing that people didn't like in Jessop. He spoke again.

'It's you novelists who're responsible, you know. You've made a world in which everyone is always falling in love – but it's not this world. Here it's the flicker of the body.

'I don't say there isn't such a thing. There is. I've seen it, but it's rare, as rare as-as-a perfect horse, an Arab once said to me. The real thing, it's too queer to be anything but the rarest; it's the queerest thing in the world. Think of it for a moment, chucking out of your mind all this business of kisses and moonlight and marriages. A miserable tailless ape buzzed round through space on this half cold cinder of an earth, a timid bewildered ignorant savage little beast always fighting for bare existence. And suddenly it runs up against another miserable naked tailless ape and immediately everything that it has ever known dies out of its little puddle of a mind, itself, its beastly body, its puny wandering desires, the wretched fight for existence, the whole world. And instead there comes a flame of passion for something in that other naked ape, not for her body or her mind or her soul, but for something beautiful mysterious everlasting – yes that's it, the everlasting passion in her which has flamed up in him. He goes buzzing on through space, but he isn't tired or bewildered or ignorant any more; he can see his way now even among the stars.

'And that's love, the love which you novelists scatter about so freely. What does it mean? I don't understand it; it's queer beyond anything I've ever struck. It isn't animal – that's the point – or vegetable or mineral. Not one man in ten thousand feels it and not one woman in twenty thousand. How can they? It's feeling, a passion immense, steady, enduring. But not one person in twenty thousand ever feels anything at all for more than a second, and then it's only a feeble ripple on the smooth surface of their unconsciousness.

'O yes, we've all been in love. We can all remember the kisses we gave and the kisses given to us in the moonlight. But that's the body. The body's damnably exacting. It wants to kiss and to be kissed at certain times and seasons. It isn't particular however; give it moonlight and young lips and it's soon satisfied. It's only when we don't pay for it that we call it romance and love, and the most we would ever pay is a £5 note.

'But it's not love, not the other, the real, the mysterious thing. That too exists, I've seen it, I tell you, but it's rare Lord, it's rare. I'm middle-aged. I've seen men, thousands of them, all over the world, known them too, made it my business to know them, it interests me, a hobby like collecting stamps. And I've only known two cases of real love.

'And neither of them had anything to do with kisses and moonlight. Why should they? When it comes, it comes in strange ways and places, like most real things perversely and unreasonably. I suppose scientifically it's all right – it's what the mathematician calls the law of chances.

'I'll tell you about one of them.

'There was a man – you may have read his books, so I won't give you his name – though he's dead now – I'll call him Reynolds. He was at Rugby with me and also at Corpus. He was a thin feeble-looking chap, very nervous, with pale face and long pale hands. He was bullied a good deal at school; he was what they call a smug. I knew him rather well; there seemed to me to be something in him somewhere, some power of feeling under nervousness and shyness. I can't say it ever came out, but he interested me.

'I went East and he stayed at home and wrote novels. I read them; very romantic they were too, the usual ideas of men and women and love. But they were clever in many ways, especially psychologically, as it was called. He was a success, he made money.

'I used to get letters from him about once in three months, so when he came travelling to the east it was arranged that he would stay a week with me. I was in Colombo at that time right in the passenger route. I found him one day on the deck of a P & O just the same as I had last seen him in Oxford, except for the large sun helmet on his head and the blue glasses on his nose. And when I got him back to the bungalow and began to talk with him on the broad verandah, I found that be was still just the same inside too. The years had not touched him anywhere, he had not in the ordinary sense lived at all. He had stood aside – do you see what I mean? – from shyness, nervousness, the remembrance and fear of being bullied, and watched other people living. He knew a good deal about how other people think, the little tricks and mannerisms of life and novels, but he didn't know how they felt; I expect he had never felt anything himself, except fear and shyness: he hadn't really ever known a man, and he had certainly never known a woman.

'Well he wanted to see life, to understand it, to feel it. He had travelled 7,000 miles to do so. He was very keen to begin, he wanted to see life all round, up and down, inside and out; he told me so as we looked out on the palm trees and the glimpse of the red road beyond and the unending stream of brown men and women upon it.

'I began to show him life in the East. I took him to the clubs, the club where they play tennis and gossip, the club where they play bridge and gossip, the club where they just sit in the long chairs and gossip. I introduced him to scores of men who asked him to have a drink and to scores of women who asked him whether he liked Colombo. He didn't get on with them at all, he said "No thank you" to the men and "Yes, very much" to the women. He was shy and felt uncomfortable, out of his element with these fat flannelled merchants, fussy civil servants, and their whining wives and daughters.

'In the evening we sat on my verandah and talked. We talked about life and his novels and romance and love even. I liked him, you know; he interested me, there was something in him which had never come out. But he had got hold of life at the wrong end somehow, he couldn't deal with it or the people in it at all. He had the novelist's view of life and – with all respect to you, Alderton – it doesn't work.

'I suppose the devil came into me that evening. Reynolds had talked so much about seeing life that at last I thought: "By Jove, I'll show him a side of life he's never seen before at any rate." I called the servant and told him to fetch two rickshaws.

'We bowled along the dusty roads past the lake and into the native quarter. All the smells of the East rose up and hung heavy upon the damp hot air in the narrow streets. I watched Reynolds' face in the moonlight, the scared look which always showed upon it; I very nearly repented and turned back. Even now I'm not sure whether I'm sorry that I didn't. At any rate I didn't, and at last we drew up in front of a low mean-looking house standing back a little from the road.

'There was one of those queer native wooden doors made in two halves; the top half was open and through it one saw an empty white-washed room lighted by a lamp fixed in the wall. We went in and I shut the door top and bottom behind us. At the other end were two steps leading up to another room. Suddenly there came the sound of bare feet running and giggles of laughter, and ten or twelve girls, some naked and some half clothed in bright red or bright orange clothes, rushed down the steps upon us. We were surrounded, embraced, caught up in their arms and carried into the next room. We lay upon sofas with them. There was nothing but sofas and an old piano in the room.

'They knew me well in the place, – you can imagine what it was – I often went there. Apart from anything else, it interested me. The girls were all Tamils and Sinhalese. It always reminded me somehow of the Arabian Nights; that room when you came into it so bare and empty, and then the sudden rush of laughter, the pale yellow naked women, the brilliant colours of the cloths, the white teeth, all appearing so suddenly in the doorway up there at the end of the room. And the girls themselves interested me; I used to sit and talk to them for hours in their own language; they didn't as a rule understand English. They used to tell me all about themselves, queer pathetic stories often. They came from villages almost always, little native villages hidden far away among rice fields and coconut trees, and they had drifted somehow into this hovel in the warren of filth and smells which we and our civilization had attracted about us.

'Poor Reynolds, he was very uncomfortable at first. He didn't know what to do in the least or where to look. He stammered out yes and no to the broken English sentences which the girls repeated like parrots to him. They soon got tired of kissing him and came over to me to tell me their little troubles and ask me for advice – all of them that is, except one.

'She was called Celestinahami and was astonishingly beautiful. Her skin was the palest of pale gold with a glow in it, very rare in the fair native women. The delicate innocent beauty of a child was in her face; and her eyes, Lord, her eyes immense, deep, dark and melancholy which looked as if they knew and understood and felt everything in the world. She never wore anything coloured, just a white cloth wrapped round her waist with one end thrown over the left shoulder. She carried about her an air of slowness and depth and mystery of silence and of innocence.

'She lay full length on the sofa with her chin on her hands, looking up into Reynolds' face and smiling at him. The white cloth had slipped down and her breasts were bare. She was a Sinhalese, a cultivator's daughter, from a little village up in the hills: her place was in the green rice fields weeding, or in the little compound under the palm trees pounding rice, but she lay on the dirty sofa and asked Reynolds in her soft broken English whether he would have a drink.

'It began in him with pity. "I saw the pity of it, Jessop," he said to me afterwards, "the pity of it". He lost his shyness, he began to talk to her in his gentle cultivated voice; she didn't understand a word, but she looked up at him with her great innocent eyes and smiled at him. He even stroked her hand and her arm. She smiled at him still, and said her few soft clipped English sentences, He looked into her eyes that understood nothing but seemed to understand everything, and then it came out at last; the power to feel, the power that so few have, the flame, the passion, love, the real thing.

'It was the real thing, I tell you; I ought to know: he stayed on in my bungalow day after day, and night after night he went down to that hovel among the filth and smells. It wasn't the body, it wasn't kisses and moonlight. He wanted her of course, he wanted her body and soul; but he wanted something else: the same passion, the same fine strong thing that he felt moving in himself. She was everything to him that was beautiful and great and pure, she was what she looked, what he read in the depths of her eyes. And she might have been – why not? She might have been all that and more, there's no reason why such a thing shouldn't happen, shouldn't have happened even. One can believe that still. But the chances are all against it. She was a prostitute in a Colombo brothel, a simple soft little golden-skinned animal with nothing in the depths of the eyes at all. It was the law of chances at work as usual, you know.

'It was tragic and it was at the same time wonderfully ridiculous. At times he saw things as they were, the bare truth, the hopelessness of it. And then he was so ignorant of life, fumbling about so curiously with all the little things in it. It was too much for him; he tried to shoot himself with a revolver which he had bought at the Army and Navy Stores before he sailed; but he couldn't because he had forgotten how to put in the cartridges.

'Yes, I burst in on him sitting at a table in his room fumbling with the thing. It was one of those rotten old-fashioned things with a piece of steel that snaps down over the chamber to prevent the cartridges falling out. He hadn't discovered how to snap it back in order to get the cartridges in. The man who sold him that revolver, instead of an automatic pistol, as he ought to have done, saved his life.

'And then I talked to him seriously. I quoted his own novel to him. It was absurdly romantic, unreal, his novel, but it preached as so many of them do, that you should face facts first and then live your life out to the uttermost. I quoted it to him. Then I told him baldly brutally what the girl was – not a bit what he thought her, what his passion went out to – a nice simple soft little animal like the bitch at my feet that starved herself if I left her for a day. "It's the truth," I said to him, "as true as that you're really in love, in love with something that doesn't exist behind those great eyes. It's dangerous, damned dangerous because it's real – and that's why it's rare. But it's no good shooting yourself with that thing. You've got to get on board the next P & O, that's what you've got to do. And if you won't do that, why practise what you preach and live your life out, and take the risks."

'He asked me what I meant.

'"The risks?" I said. "I can see what they are, and if you do take them, you're taking the worst odds ever offered a man. But there they are. Take the girl and see what you can make of life with her. You can buy her out of that place for fifteen rupees."

'I was wrong, I suppose. I ought to have put him in irons and shipped him off next day. But I don't know, really I don't know.

'He took the risks any way. We bought her out, it cost twenty rupees. I got them a little house down the coast on the seashore, a little house surrounded by palm trees. The sea droned away sleepily right under the verandah. It was to be an idyll of the East; he was to live there for ever with her and write novels on the verandah.

'And, by God, he was happy – at first. I used to go down there and stay with them pretty often. He taught her English and she taught him Sinhalese. He started to write a novel about the East: it would have been a good novel I think, full of strength und happiness and sun and reality – if it had been finished. But it never was. He began to see the truth, the damned hard un-pleasant truths that I had told him that night in the Colombo bungalow. And the cruelty of it was that he still had that rare power to feel, that he still felt. It was the real thing, you see, and the real thing is – didn't I say – immense, steady, enduring. It is; I believe that still. He was in love, but he knew now what she was like. He couldn't speak to her and she couldn't speak to him, she couldn't understand him. He was a civilized cultivated intelligent nervous little man and she – she was an animal, dumb and stupid and beautiful.

'I watched it happening, I had foretold it, but I cursed myself for not having stopped it, scores of times. He loved her but she tortured him. People would say, I suppose, that she got on his nerves. It's a good enough description. But the cruellest thing of all was that she had grown to love him, love him like an animal, as a bitch loves her master.' Jessop stopped. We waited for him to go on but he didn't. The leaves rustled gently in the breeze: the river murmured softly below us; up in the woods I heard a nightingale singing. 'Well, and then ?' Alderton asked at last in a rather peevish voice.

'And then? Damn that nightingale!' said Jessop. 'I wish I hadn't begun this story. It happened so long ago: I thought I had forgotten to feel it, to feel that I was responsible for what happened then. There's another sort of love; it isn't the body and it isn't the flame, it's the love of dogs and women, at any rate of those slow, big-eyed women of the East. It's the love of a slave, the patient, consuming love for a master, for his kicks and his caresses, for his kisses and his blows. That was the sort of love which grew up slowly in Celestinahami for Reynolds. But it wasn't what he wanted, it was that, I expect, more than anything which got on his nerves.

'She used to follow him about the bungalow like a dog. He wanted to talk to her about his novel and she only understood how to pound and cook rice. It exasperated him, made him unkind, cruel. And when he looked into her patient. mysterious eyes he saw behind them what he had fallen in love with, what he knew didn't exist. It began to drive him mad.

'And she – she of course couldn't even understand what was the matter. She saw that he was unhappy, she thought she had done something wrong. She reasoned like a child that it was because she wasn't like the white ladies whom she used to see in Colombo. So she went and bought stays and white cotton stockings and shoes, and she squeezed herself into them. But the stays and the shoes and stockings didn't do her any good.

'It couldn't go on like that. At last I induced Reynolds to go away. He was to continue his travels but he was coming back – he said so over and over again to me and to Celestinahami. Meanwhile she was well provided for; a deed was executed: the house and the coconut trees and the little compound by the sea were to be hers – a generous settlement, a *donatio inter vivos*, as the lawyers call it – void, eh? – or voidable? – because for an immoral consideration. Lord! I'm nearly forgetting my law, but I believe the law holds that only future consideration of that sort can be immoral. How wise, how just, isn't it? The past cannot be immoral; it's done with, wiped out – but the future? Yes, it's only the future that counts.

'So Reynolds wiped out his past and Celestinahami by the help of a dirty Burgher lawyer and a deed of gift and a ticket issued by Thomas Cook and Son for a berth in a P & O bound for Aden. I went on board to see him off and I shook his hand and told him encouragingly that everything would be all right.

'I never saw Reynolds again but I saw Celestinahami once. It was at the inquest two days after the Moldavia sailed for Aden. She was lying on a dirty wooden board on trestles in the dingy mud-plastered room behind the court. Yes, I identified her: Celestinahami – I never knew her other name. She lay there in her stays and pink skirt and white stockings and white shoes. They had found her floating in the sea that lapped the foot of the convent garden below the little bungalow – bobbing up and down in her stays and pink skirt and white stockings and shoes.'

Jessop stopped. No one spoke for a minute or two. Then Hanson Smith stretched himself, yawned, and got up.

'Battle, murder, and sentimentality,' he said. 'You're as bad as the rest of them, Jessop. I'd like to hear your other case – but it's too late, I'm off to bed.'

Pearls and Swine

I had finished my hundred up[1] – or rather he had – with the Colonel and we strolled into the smoking room for a smoke and a drink round the fire before turning in. There were three other men already round the fire and they widened their circle to take us in. I didn't know them, hadn't spoken to them or indeed to anyone except the Colonel in the large gaudy uncomfortably comfortable hotel. I was run down, out of sorts generally, and – like a fool, I thought now – had taken a week off to eat, or rather to read the menus of interminable table d'hote dinners, to play golf and to walk on the 'front' at Torquay.

I had only arrived the day before, but the Colonel (retired) a jolly tubby little man – with white moustaches like two S's lying side by side on the top of his stupid red lips and his kind choleric eyes bulging out on a life which he was quite content never for a moment to understand – made it a point, my dear Sir, to know every new arrival within one hour after he arrived.

We got our drinks and as, rather forgetting that I was in England, I murmured the Eastern formula, I noticed vaguely one of the other three glance at me over his shoulder for a moment. The Colonel stuck out his fat little legs in front of him, turning up his neatly shoed toes before the blaze. Two of the others were talking, talking as men so often do in the comfortable chairs of smoking rooms between ten and eleven at night, earnestly, seriously, of what they call affairs, or politics or questions. I listened to their fat, full-fed assured voices in that heavy room which smelt of solidity, safety, horsehair furniture, tobacco smoke, and the faint civilized aroma of whisky and soda. It came as a shock to me in that atmosphere that they were discussing India and the East: it does you know every now and again. Sentimental? Well, I expect one is sentimental about it, having lived there. It doesn't seem to go with solidity and horsehair furniture: the fifteen years come back to one in one moment all in a heap. How one hated it and how one loved it!

I suppose they had started on the Durbar and the King's visit. They had got on to Indian unrest, to our position in India, its duties, responsibilities, to the problem of East and West. They hadn't been there of course, they hadn't even seen the brothel and cafe chantant at Port Said suddenly open out into that pink and blue desert that leads you through Africa and Asia into the heart of the East. But they knew all about it, they had solved, with their fat voices and in their fat heads, riddles, older than the Sphinx, of peoples remote and ancient and mysterious whom they had never seen and could never understand. One was, I imagine, a stock-jobber, plump and comfortable with a greasy forehead and a high colour in his cheeks, smooth shiny brown hair and a carefully grown small moustache: a good dealer in the market: sharp and confident, with a loud voice and shifty eyes. The other was a clergyman: need I say more? Except that he was more of a clergyman even than most clergymen, I mean that he wore tight things – leggings don't they call them? or breeches? – round his calves. I never know what it means: whether they are bishops or rural deans or archdeacons or archimandrites. In any case I mistrust them even more than the black trousers: they seem to close the last door for anything human to get in through the black clothes. The dog collar closes up the armour above, and below, as long as they *were* trousers, at any rate some whiff of humanity might have eddied up the legs of them and touched bare flesh. But the gaiters button them up finally, irremediably, for ever.

I expect he was an archdeacon; he was saying: 'You can't impose Western civilization upon an Eastern people – I believe I'm right in saying that there are over two hundred millions in our Indian Empire – without a little disturbance. I'm a Liberal you know. I've been a Liberal my whole life – family tradition – though I grieve to say I could not follow Mr. Gladstone on the Home Rule question. It seems to me a good sign, this movement, an awakening among the people. But don't misunderstand me, my dear Sir, I am not making any excuses for the methods of the extremists. Apart from my calling – I have a natural horror of violence. Nothing can condone violence, the taking of human life, it's savagery, terrible, terrible.'

'They don't put it down with a strong enough hand,' the stock-jobber was saying almost fiercely. 'There's too much Liberalism in the East, too much namby-pambyism. It is all right here, of course, but it's not suited to the East. They want a strong hand. After all they owe us something: we aren't going to take all the kicks and leave them all the halfpence. Rule 'em, I say, rule 'em, if you're going to rule 'em. Look after 'em, of course: give 'em schools, if they want education – schools, hospitals, roads, and railways. Stamp out the plague, fever, famine. But let 'em know you are top dog. That's the way to run an eastern country. I am a white man, you're black; I'll treat you well, give you courts and justice; but I'm the superior race, I'm master here.'

The man who had looked round at me when I said 'Here's luck!' was fidgeting about in his chair uneasily. I examined him more carefully. There was no mistaking the cause of his irritation. It was written on his face, the small close-cut white moustache, the smooth firm cheeks with the red-and-brown glow on them, the innumerable wrinkles round the eyes, and above all the eyes themselves, that had grown slow and steady and unastonished, watching that inexplicable, meaningless march of life under blazing suns. He had seen it, he knew. 'Ah,' I thought, 'he is beginning to feel his liver. If he would only begin to speak, we might have some fun.'

H'm, h'm, said the archdeacon. 'Of course there's something in what you say. Slow and sure. Things may be going too fast, and, as I say, I'm entirely for putting down violence and illegality with a strong hand. And after all, my dear Sir, when you say we're the superior race you imply a duty. Even in secular matters we must spread the light. I believe – devoutly – I am not ashamed to say so – that we are. We're reaching the people there, it's the cause of the unrest, we set them an example. They desire to follow. Surely, surely we should help to guide their feet. I don't speak without a certain knowledge. I take a great interest, I may even say that I play my small part, in the work of one of our great missionary societies. I see our young men, many of them risen from the people, educated often, and highly educated (I venture to think), in Board Schools. I see them go out full of high ideals to live among those poor people. And I see them when they come back and tell me their tales honestly, unostentatiously. It is always the same, a message of hope and comfort. We are getting at the people, by example, by our lives, by our conduct. They respect us.'

I heard a sort of groan, and then quite loud, these strange words: 'Kasimutal Rameswaramvaraiyil terintavan.'

'I beg your pardon,' said the Archdeacon, turning to the interrupter.

'I beg yours. Tamil, Tamil, proverb. Came into my mind. Spoke without thinking. Beg yours.'

'Not at all. Very interesting. You've lived in India? Would you mind my asking you for a translation ?'

'It means "he knows everything between Benares and Rameswaram". Last time I heard it, an old Tamil, seventy or eighty years old, perhaps – he looked a hundred – used it of one of your young men. The young man, by the bye, had been a year and a half in India. D'you understand ?'

'Well, I'm not sure I do: I've heard, of course, of Benares, but Rameswaram, I don't seem to remember the name.'

I laughed; I could not help it; the little Anglo-Indian looked so fierce, 'Ah!' he said, 'you don't recollect the name. Well, it's pretty famous out there. Great temple – Hindu – right at the southern tip of India. Benares, you know, is up north. The old Tamil meant that your friend knew everything in India after a year and a half: *he* didn't you know, after seventy, after seven thousand years. Perhaps you also don't recollect that the Tamils are Dravidians? They've been there since the beginning of time, before we came, or the Dutch or Portuguese or the Muhammadans, or our cousins, the other Aryans. Uncivilized, black? Perhaps, but, if they're black, after all it's *their* suns, through thousands of years, that have blackened them. They ought to know, if anyone does: but they don't, they don't pretend to. But you two gentlemen, you seem to know everything between Kasimutal – that's Benares – and Rameswaram, without having seen the sun at all.'

'My dear Sir,' began the Archdeacon pompously, but the jobber interrupted him. He had had a number of whiskies and sodas, and was quite heated. 'It's very easy to sneer: it doesn't mean because you've lived a few years in a place...'

'I? Thirty. But they – seven thousand at least.'

'I say, it doesn't mean because you've lived thirty years in a place that you know all about it. Ramisram, or whatever the damned place is called, I've never heard of it and don't want to. You do, that's part of your job, I expect. But I read the papers, I've read books too, mind you, about India. I know what's going on. One knows enough – enough – data: East and West and the difference: I can form an opinion – I've a right to it even if I've never heard of Ramis what d'you call it. You've lived there and you can't see the wood for the trees. We see it because we're out of it – see it at a distance.'

'Perhaps,' said the Archdeacon 'there's a little misunderstanding. The discussion – if I may say so – is getting a little heated – unnecessarily, I think. We hold our views. This gentleman has lived in the country. He holds others. I'm sure it would be most interesting to hear them. But I confess I didn't quite gather them from what he said.'

The little man was silent: he sat back, his eyes fixed on the ceiling. Then he smiled.

'I won't give you views,' he said. 'But if you like I'll give you what you call details, things seen, facts. Then you can give me *your* views on 'em.'

They murmured approval.

'Let's see, it's fifteen, seventeen years ago. I had a district then about as big as England. There may have been twenty Europeans in it, counting the missionaries, and twenty million Tamils and Telegus. I expect nineteen million of the Tamils and Telegus never saw a white man from one year's end to the other, or if they did, they caught a glimpse of me under a sun helmet riding through their village on a flea-bitten grey Indian mare. Well, Providence had so designed it that there was a stretch of coast in that district which was a barren wilderness of sand and scrubby thorn jungle – and nothing else – for three hundred miles; no towns, no villages, no water, just sand and trees for three hundred miles. O, and sun, I forget that, blazing sun. And in the water off the shore at one place there were oysters, millions of them lying and breeding at the bottom, four or five fathoms down. And in the oysters, or some of them, were pearls.

'Well, we rule India and the sea, so the sea belongs to us, and the oysters are in the sea and the pearls are in the oysters. Therefore of course the pearls belong to us. But they lie in five fathoms. How to get 'em up, that's the question. You'd think being progressive we'd dredge for them or send down divers in diving dresses. But we don't, not in India. They've been fishing up the oysters and the pearls there ever since the beginning of time, naked brown men diving feet first out of long wooden boats into the blue sea and sweeping the oysters off the bottom of the sea into baskets slung to their sides. They were doing it centuries and centuries before we came, when – as someone said – our ancestors were herding swine on the plains of Norway.

The Arabs of the Persian Gulf came down in dhows and fished up pearls which found their way to Solomon and the Queen of Sheba. They still come, and the Tamils and Moormen of the district come, and they fish 'em up in the same way, diving out of long wooden boats shaped and rigged as in Solomon's time, as they were centuries before him and the Queen of Sheba. No difference, you see, except that we – Government I mean – take two-thirds of all the oysters fished up: the other third we give to the diver, Arab or Tamil or Moorman, for his trouble in fishing 'em up.

'We used to have a Pearl Fishery about once in three years, it lasted six weeks or two months just between the two monsoons, the only time the sea is calm there. And I had, of course, to go and superintend it, to take Government's share of oysters, to sell them, to keep order, to keep out K.D.'s – that means Known Depredators – and smallpox and cholera. We had what we called a camp, in the wilderness remember, on the hot sand down there by the sea: it sprang up in a night, a town, a big town of thirty or forty thousand people, a little India, Asia almost, even a bit of Africa. They came from all districts: Tamils, Telegus, fat Chetties, Parsees, Bombay merchants, Sinhalese from Ceylon, the Arabs and their negroes, Somalis probably, who used to be their slaves. It was an immense gamble; everyone bought oysters for the chance of the prizes in them: it would have taken fifty white men to superintend that camp properly: they gave me one, a little boy of twenty-four fresh-cheeked from England, just joined the service. He had views, he had been educated in a Board School, won prizes, scholarships, passed the Civil Service 'Exam.' Yes, he had views; he used to explain them to me when he first arrived. He got some new ones I think before he got out of that camp. You'd say he only saw details, things happen, facts, data. Well, he did that too. He saw men die – he hadn't seen that in his Board School – die of plague or cholera, like flies, all over the place, under the trees, in the boats, outside the little door of his own little hut. And he saw flies, too, millions, billions of them all day long buzzing, crawling over everything, his hands, his little fresh face, his food. And he smelt the smell of millions of decaying oysters all day long and all night long for six weeks. He was sick four or five times a day for six weeks; the smell did that. Insanitary? Yes, very. Why is it allowed? The pearls, you see, the pearls: you must get them out of the oysters as you must get the oysters out of the sea. And the pearls are very often small and embedded in the oyster's body. So you put all the oysters, millions of them, in dug-out canoes in the sun to rot. They rot very well in that sun, and the flies come and lay eggs in them, and maggots come out of the eggs and more flies come out of the maggots; and between them all, the maggots and the sun, the oysters' bodies disappear, leaving the pearls and a little sand at the bottom of the canoe. Unscientific? Yes, perhaps; but after all it's our camp, our fishery, – just as it was in Solomon's time? At any rate, you see, it's the East. But whatever it is, and whatever the reason, the result involves flies, millions of them and a smell, a stench – Lord! I can smell it now.

'There was one other white man there. He was a planter, so he said, and he had come to 'deal' in pearls. He dropped in on us out of a native boat at sunset on the second day. He had a red face and a red nose, he was unhealthily fat for the East: the whites of his eyes were rather blue and rather red: they were also watery. I noticed that his hand shook, and that he first refused and then took a whisky and soda – a bad sign in the East. He wore very dirty white clothes and a vest instead of a shirt: he apparently had no baggage of any sort. But he was a white man, and so he ate with us that night and a good many nights afterwards.

'In the second week he had his first attack of D.T.[2] We pulled him through, Robson and I, in the intervals of watching over the oysters. When he hadn't got D.T., he talked: he was a great talker, he also had views. I used to sit in the evenings – they were rare – when the fleet of boats had got in early and the oysters had been divided, in front of my hut and listen to him and Robson settling India and Asia, Africa too probably. We sat there in our long chairs on the sand looking out over the purple sea, towards a sunset like blood shot with gold. Nothing moved or stirred except the flies which were going to sleep in a mustard tree close by; they hung in buzzing clusters, billions of them on the smooth leaves and little twigs: literally it was black with them. It looked as if the whole tree had suddenly broken out all over into some disease of living black currants. Even the sea seemed to move with an effort in the hot, still air; only now and again a little wave would lift itself up very slowly, very wearily, poise itself for a moment, and then fall with a weary little thud on the sand.

'I used to watch them, I say, in the hot still air and the smell of dead oysters – it pushed up against your face like something solid talking, talking in their long chairs, while the sweat stood out in little drops on their foreheads and trickled from time to time down their noses. There wasn't, I suppose, anything wrong with Robson, he was all right at bottom, but he annoyed me, irritated me in that smell. He was too cocksure altogether, of himself, of his Board School education, of life, of his "views." He was going to run India on new lines laid down in some damned Manual of Political Science out of which they learn life in Board Schools and extension lectures. He would run his own life, I dare say, on the same lines, laid down in some other text book or primer. He hadn't seen anything, but he knew exactly what it was all like. There was nothing curious, astonishing, unexpected, in life, he was ready for any emergency. And we were all wrong, all on the wrong tack in dealing with natives! He annoyed me a little, you know, when the thermometer stood at 99, at 6 p.m., but what annoyed me still more was that they – the natives! – were all wrong too. They too had to be taught how to live – and die, too, I gathered.

'But his views were interesting, very interesting – especially in the long chairs there under the immense Indian sky, with the camp at our hands – just as it had been in the time of Moses and Abraham – and behind us the jungle for miles, and behind that India, three hundred millions of them listening to the piping voice of a Board School boy, are the inferior race, these three hundred millions – mark race, though there are more races in India than people in Peckham – and we, of course, are superior. They've stopped somehow on the bottom rung of the ladder of which we've very nearly, if not quite, reached the top. They've stopped there hundreds, thousands of years: but it won't take any time to lead 'em up by the hand to our rung. It's to be done like this: by showing them that they're our brothers, inferior brothers; by reason, arguing them out of their superstitions, false beliefs; by education by science, by example, yes, even he did not forget example, and White, sitting by his side with his red nose and watery eyes, nodded approval. And all this must be done scientifically, logically, systematically: if it were, a Commissioner could revolutionize a province in five years, turn it into a Japanese India, with all the ryots as well as all the vakils[3] and students running up the ladder of European civilization to become, I suppose, glorified Board School angels at the top. "But you've none of you got clear plans out here," he piped, "you never work on any system; you've got no point of view. The result is" – here, I think, he was inspired, by the dead oysters, perhaps – "instead of getting hold of the East, it's the East which gets hold of you."

'And White agreed with him, solemnly, at any rate when he was sane and sober. And I couldn't complain of his inexperience. He was rather reticent at first, but afterwards we heard much – too much – of his experiences – one does, when a man gets D.T. He said he was a gentleman, and I believe it was true; he had been to a public school; Cheltenham or Repton. He hadn't, I gathered, succeeded as a gentleman at home, so they sent him to travel in the East. He liked it, it suited him. So he became a planter in Assam. That was fifteen years ago, but he didn't like Assam: the luck was against him – it always was – and he began to roll; and when a man starts rolling in India, well – He had been a clerk in merchants' offices; he had served in a draper's shop in Calcutta; but the luck was always against him. Then he tramped up and down India, through Ceylon, Burma; he had got at one time or another to the Malay States, and when he was very bad one day, he talked of cultivating camphor in Java. He had been a sailor on a coasting tramp; he had sold horses (which didn't belong to him) in the Deccan somewhere; he had tramped day after day begging his way for months in native bazaars; he had lived for six months with, and on, a Tamil woman in some little village down in the south. Now he was "dealing in" pearls. "India's got hold of me," he'd say, "India's got hold of me and the East."

'He had views too, very much like Robson's, with additions. "The strong hand" came in, and "rule". We ought to govern India more; we didn't now. Why, he had been in hundreds of places where he was the first Englishman that the people had ever seen. (Lord! think of that!). He talked a great deal about the hidden wealth of India and exploitation. He knew places where there was gold – workable too – only one wanted a little capital – coal probably and iron – and then there was this new stuff, radium. But we weren't go-ahead, progressive, the Government always put difficulties in his way. They made "the native" their stalking-horse against European enterprise. He would work for the good of the native, he'd treat him firmly but kindly – especially, I thought, the native women, for his teeth were sharp and pointed and there were spaces between each, and there was something about his chin and jaw – you know the type, I expect.

'As the fishing went on we had less time to talk. We had to work. The divers go out in the fleet of three hundred or four hundred boats every night and dive until midday. Then they sail back from the pearl banks and bring all their oysters into an immense Government enclosure where the Government share is taken. If the wind is favourable all the boats got back by 6 p.m. and the work is over at 7. But if the wind starts blowing off shore, the fleet gets scattered and boats drop in one by one all night long. Robson and I had to be in the enclosure as long as there was a boat out, ready to see that, as soon as it did get in, the oysters were brought to the enclosure and Government got its share.

'Well, the wind never did blow favourably that year. I sat in that enclosure sometimes for forty-eight hours on end. Robson found managing it rather difficult, so he didn't like to be left there alone. If you get two thousand Arabs, Tamils, Negroes, and Moormen, each with a bag or two of oysters, into an enclosure a hundred and fifty yards by a hundred and fifty yards, and you only have thirty timid native 'subordinates' and twelve native policemen to control them – well, somehow or other he found a difficulty in applying his system of reasoning to them. The first time he tried it, we very nearly had a riot; it arose from a dispute between some Arabs and Tamils over the ownership of three oysters which fell out of a bag. The Arabs didn't understand Tamil and the Tamils didn't understand Arabic, and, when I got down there, fetched by a frightened constable, there were sixty or seventy men fighting with great poles – they had pulled up the fence of the enclosure for weapons – and on the outskirts was Robson running round like a distracted hen with a white face and tears in his blue eyes. When we got the combatants separated, they had only killed one Tamil and broken nine or ten heads. Robson was very upset by that dead Tamil, he broke down utterly for a minute or two, I'm afraid.

'Then White got his second attack. He was very bad: he wanted to kill himself, but was worse than that, before killing himself, he wanted to kill other people. I hadn't been to bed for two nights and I knew I should have to sit up another night in that enclosure as the wind was all wrong again. I had given White a bed in my hut: it wasn't good to let him wander in the bazaar. Robson came down with a white face to tell me he had "gone mad up there again." I had to knock him down with the butt end of a rifle; he was a big man and I hadn't slept for forty-eight hours, and then there were the flies and the smell of those dead oysters.

'It sounds unreal, perhaps a nightmare, all this told here to you behind blinds and windows in this –' he sniffed – 'in this smell of – of – horsehair furniture and paint and varnish. The curious thing is it didn't seem a nightmare out there. It was too real. Things happened, anything might happen, without shocking or astonishing. One just did one's work, hour after hour, keeping things going in that sun which stung one's bare hands, took the skin off even my face, among the flies and the smell. It wasn't a nightmare, it was just a few thousand Arabs and Indians fishing up oysters from the bottom of the sea. It wasn't even new, one felt; it was old, old as the Bible, old as Adam, so the Arabs said. One hadn't much time to think, but one felt it and watched it, watched the things happen quietly, unastonished, as men do in the East. One does one's work, – forty-eight hours at a stretch doesn't leave one much time or inclination for thinking, – waiting for things to happen. If you can prevent people from killing one another or robbing one another, or burning down the camp, or getting cholera or plague or small-pox, and if one can manage to get one night's sleep in three, one is fairly satisfied; one doesn't much worry about having to knock a mad gentleman from Repton on the head with the butt end of a rifle between-whiles.

'I expect that's just what Robson would call "not getting hold of India but letting India get hold of you". Well, I said I wouldn't give you views and I won't: I'm giving you facts: what I want, you know, too, is to give you the feeling of facts out there. After all that is data for your views, isn't it? Things here feel so different; you seem so far from life, with windows and blinds and curtains always in between, and then nothing ever happens, you never wait for things to happen, never watch things happening here. You are always doing things somehow – Lord knows what they are – according I suppose to systems, views, opinions. But out there you live so near to life, every morning you smell damp earth if you splash too much in your tin bath. And things happen slowly, inexorably by fate, and you – you don't do things, you watch with the three hundred millions. You feel it there in every-thing, even in the sunrise and sunset, every day, the immensity, inexorableness, mystery of things happening. You feel the whole earth waking up or going to sleep in a great arch of sky; you feel small, not very powerful. But who ever felt the sun set or rise in London or Torquay either? It doesn't: you just turn on or turn off the electric light.

'White was very bad that night. When he recovered from being knocked down by the rifle, I had to tie him down to the bed. And then Robson broke down – nerves, you know. I had to go back to the enclosure and I wanted him to stay and look after White in the hut – it wasn't safe to leave him alone even tied down with cord to the camp bed. But this was apparently another emergency to which the manual system did not apply. He couldn't face it alone in the hut with that man tied to the bed. White was certainly not a pretty sight writhing about there, and his face – have you ever seen a man in the last stages of D.T.? I beg your pardon. I suppose you haven't. It isn't nice, and White was also seeing things, not nice either: not snakes you know as people do in novels when they get D.T., but things which had happened to him, and things which he had done – they weren't nice either – and curious ordinary things distorted in a most unpleasant way. He was very much troubled by snipe: hundreds of them kept on rising out of the bed from beside him with that shrill "cheep! cheep!" of theirs: he felt their soft little feathered bodies against his bare skin as they fluttered up from under him somewhere and flew out of the window. It threw him into paroxysms of fear, agonies: it made one, I admit, feel chilly round the heart to hear him pray to stop it.

'And Robson was also not a nice sight. I hate seeing a sane man break down with fear, mere abject fear. He just sat down at last on a cane-bottomed chair and cried like a baby. Well, that did him some good, but he wasn't fit to be left alone with White. I had to take White down to the enclosure, and I tied him to a post with coir rope near the table at which I sat there. There was nothing else to do. And Robson came too and sat there at my side through the night watching White, terrified but fascinated.

'Can you picture that enclosure to yourself down on the sandy shore with its great fence of rough poles cut in the jungle, lighted by a few flares, torches dipped in coconut oil: and the white man tied to a pole raving, writhing in the flickering light which just showed too Robson's white scared little face? And in the intervals of taking over oysters and settling disputes between Arabs and Somalis and Tamils and Moormen, I sat at the table writing a report (which had to go by runner next morning) on a proposal to introduce the teaching of French in "English schools" in towns. That wasn't a very good report. White gave us the whole history of his life between ten p.m. and four a.m. in the morning. He didn't leave much to the imagination; a parson would have said that in that hour the memory of his sins came upon him – O, I beg your pardon. But really

I think they did. I thought I had lived long enough out there to have heard without a shock anything that men can do and do – especially white men who have "gone under." But I hadn't: I couldn't stomach the story of White's life told by himself. It wasn't only that he had robbed and swindled himself through India up and down for fifteen years. That was bad enough for there wasn't a station where he hadn't swindled and bamboozled his fellow white men. But it was what he had done when he got away "among the natives" – to men, and women too, away from "civilization," in the jungle villages and high up in the mountains. God! the cold, civilized, corrupted cruelty of it. I told you, I think, that his teeth were pointed and spaced out in his month.

'And his remorse was the most horrible thing, tied to that post there, writhing under the flickering light of the flare: the remorse of fear – fear of punishment, of what was coming of death, of the horrors, real horrors and the phantom horrors of madness.

'Often during the night there was nothing to be heard in the enclosure but his screams, curses, hoarse whispers of fear. We seemed alone there in the vast stillness of the sky: only now and then a little splash from the sea down on the shore. And then would come a confused murmur from the sea and a little later perhaps the wailing voice of one man calling to another from boat to boat across the water "Abdulla! Abdulla!" And I would go out on to the shore. There were boats, ten fifteen, twenty, perhaps, coming in from the banks, sad, mysterious, in the moonlight, gliding in with the little splashings of the great round oars. Except for the slow moving of the oars one would have thought they were full of the dead, there was not a movement on board, until the boats touched the sand. Then the dark shadows, which lay like dead men about the boats, would leap into life – there would rise a sudden din of hoarse voices, shouting, calling, quarrelling. The boats swarmed with shadows running about, gesticulating, staggering under sacks of oysters, dropping one after the other over the boats' sides into the sea. The sea was full of them and soon the shore too, Arabs, Negroes, Tamils, bowed under the weight of the sacks. They came up dripping from the sea. They burst with a roar into the enclosure: they flung down their sacks of oysters with a crash. The place was full of swaying struggling forms: of men calling to one another in their different tongues: of the smell of the sea.

'And above everything one could hear the screams and prayers of the madman writhing at the post. They gathered about him, stared at him. The light of the flares fell on their dark faces, shining and dripping from the sea. They looked calm, impassive, stern. It shone too on the circle of eyes: one saw the whites of them all round him: they seemed to be judging him, weighing him: calm patient eyes of men who watched unastonished the procession of things. The Tamils' squat black figures, nearly naked, watched him silently, almost carelessly. The Arabs in their long, dirty, night-shirts, black-bearded, discussed him earnestly together with their guttural voices. Only an enormous negro, towering up to six feet six at least above the crowd, dressed in sacks and an enormous ulster, with ten copper coffee pots slung over his back and a pipe made of a whole coconut with an iron tube stuck in it in his hand, stood smiling mysteriously.

'And White thought they weren't real, that they were devils of Hell sent to plague and torture him. He cursed them, whispered at them, howled with fear. I had to explain to them that the Sahib was not well, that the sun had touched him, that they must move away. They understood. They salaamed quietly, and moved away slowly, dignified.

'I don't know how many times this didn't happen during the night. But towards morning White began to grow very weak. He moaned perpetually. Then he began to be troubled by the flesh.

As dawn showed grey in the east, he was suddenly shaken by convulsions horrible to see. He screamed for someone to bring him a woman, and, as he screamed, his head fell back: he was dead. I cut the cords quickly in a terror of haste, and covered the horror of the face. Robson was sitting in a heap in his chair. He was sobbing, his face in his hands.

'At that moment I was told I was wanted on the shore. I went quickly. The sea looked cold and grey under the faint light from the east. A cold little wind just ruffled the surface of the water. A solitary boat stood out black against the sky, just throbbing slowly up and down on the water close in shore. They had a dead Arab on board, he had died suddenly while diving, they wanted my permission to bring the body ashore. Four men waded out to the boat: the corpse was lifted out and placed upon their shoulders. They waded back slowly: the feet of the dead man stuck out, toes pointing up, very stark over the shoulders of the men in front. The body was laid on the sand. The bearded face of the dead man looked very calm, very dignified in the faint light. An Arab, his brother, sat down upon the sand near his head. He covered himself with sackcloth. I heard him weeping. It was very silent, very cold and still on the shore in the early dawn.

'A tall figure stepped forward, it was the Arab sheik, the leader of the boat. He laid his hand on the head of the weeping man and spoke to him calmly, eloquently, compassionately. I didn't understand Arabic, but I could understand what he was saying. The dead man had lived, had worked, had died. He had died working, without suffering, as men should desire to die. He had left a son behind him. The speech went on calmly, eloquently, I heard continually the word Khallas – all is over, finished. I watched the figures outlined against the grey sky – the long lean outline of the corpse with the toes sticking up so straight and stark, the crouching huddled figure of the weeping man and the tall upright sheik standing by his side. They were motionless, sombre, mysterious, part of the grey sea, of the grey sky.

'Suddenly the dawn broke red in the sky. The sheik stopped, motioned silently to the four men. They lifted the dead man on to their shoulders. They moved away down the shore by the side of the sea which began to stir under the cold wind. By their side walked the sheik, his hand laid gently on the brother's arm. I watched them move away, silent, dignified. And over the shoulders of the men I saw the feet of the dead man with the toes sticking up straight and stark.

'Then I moved away too, to make arrangements for White's burial: it had to be done at once.'

There was silence in the smoking-room. I looked round. The Colonel had fallen asleep with his mouth open. The jobber tried to look bored, the Archdeacon was, apparently, rather put out.

'It's too late, I think,' said the Archdeacon, 'to – Dear me, dear me, past one o'clock.' He got up. 'Don't you think you've chosen rather exceptional circumstances, out of the ordinary case?'

The Commissioner was looking into the few red coals that were all that was left of the fire.

'There's another Tamil proverb,' he said: 'When the cat puts his head into a pot, he thinks all is darkness.'

The Two Brahmans

Yalpanam is a very large town in the north of Ceylon; but nobody who suddenly found himself in it would believe this. Only in two or three streets is there any bustle or stir of people. It is like a gigantic village that for centuries has slept and grown, and sleeps and grows, under a forest of coconut trees and fierce sun. All the streets are the same, dazzling dusty roads between high fences made of the dried leaves of the coconut palms. Behind the fences, and completely hidden by them, are the compounds; and in the compounds still more hidden under the palms and orange and lime trees are the huts and houses of the Tamils who live there.

The north of the town lies, as it has lain for centuries, sleeping by the side of the blue lagoon, and there is a hut standing now in a compound by the side of the lagoon, where it had stood for centuries. In this hut there lived a man called Chellaya who was by caste a Brahman, and in the compound next to Chellaya's lived another Brahman called Chittampalam, and in all the other 50 or 60 compounds around them lived other Brahmans. They belonged to the highest of all castes in Yalpanam: and they could not eat food with or touch or marry into any other caste, nor could they carry earth on their heads or work at any trade, without being defiled or losing caste. Therefore all the Brahmans live together in this quarter of the town, so that they may not be defiled but may marry off their sons and daughters to daughters and sons of other Brahmans. Chellaya and Chittampalam and all the Brahmans knew that they and their fathers and their fathers' fathers had lived in the same way by the side of the blue lagoon under the palm trees for many thousands of years. They did no work, for there was no need to work. The dhobi or washer caste man, who washed the clothes of Brahmans and of no other caste, washed their white cloths and in return was given rice and allowed to be present at weddings and funerals. And there was the barber caste man who shaved the Brahmans and no other caste. And half a mile from their compounds were their Brahman rice fields in which Chellaya and each of the other Brahmans had shares; some shares had descended to them from their fathers and their grandfathers and great-grandfathers and so on from the first Brahmans, and other shares had been brought to them as dowry with their wives. These fields were sown twice a year, and the work of cultivation was done by Mukkuwa caste men. This is a custom, that Mukkuwa caste men cultivate the rice fields of Brahmans, and it had been a custom for many thousands of years.

Chellaya was forty-five and Chittampalam was forty-two, and they had lived, as all Brahmans lived, in the houses in which they had been born. There can be no doubt that quite suddenly one of the gods, or rather devils, laid a spell upon these two compounds. And this is how it happened.

Chellaya had married, when he was 14, a plump Brahman girl of 12 who had borne him three sons and two daughters. He had married off both his daughters without giving very large dowries and his sons had all married girls who had brought them large dowries. No man ought to have been happier, though his wife was too talkative and had a sharp tongue. And for 45 years Chellaya lived happily the life which all good Brahmans should live. Every morning he ate his rice cakes and took his bath at the well in his compound and went to the temple of Siva. There he talked until midday to his wife's brother and his daughter's husband's father about Nallatampi, their neighbour, who was on bad terms with them, about the price of rice, and about a piece of land which he had been thinking of buying for the last five years. After the midday meal of rice and curry, cooked by his wife, he dozed through the afternoon; and then, when the sun began to lose its power, he went down to the shore of the blue lagoon and sat there until nightfall.

This was Chellaya's passion, to sit by the side of the still, shining, blue waters and look over them at the far-off islands which flickered and quivered in the mirage of heat. The wind, dying down at evening, just murmured in the palms behind him. The heat lay like something tangible and soothing upon the earth. And Chellaya waited eagerly for the hour when the fishermen come out with their cast-nets and wade out into the shallow water after the fish. How eagerly he waited all day for that moment; even in the temple when talking about Nallatampi, whom he hated, the vision of those unruffled waters would continually rise up before him, and of the lean men lifting their feet so gently first one and then the other, in order not to make a splash or a ripple, and bending forward with the nets in their hands ready to cast. And then the joy of the capture, the great leaping twisting silver fish in the net at last. He began to hate his compound and his fat wife and the interminable talk in the temple, and those long dreary evenings when he stood under his umbrella at the side of his rice field and watched the Mukkuwas ploughing or sowing or reaping.

As Chellaya grew older he became more and more convinced that the only pleasure in life was to be a fisher and to catch fish. This troubled him not a little, for the Fisher caste is a low caste and no Brahman had ever caught a fish. It would be utter pollution and losing of caste to him. One day however when he went down to sit in his accustomed place by the side of the lagoon, he found a fisherman sitting on the sand there mending his net.

'Fisher,' said Chellaya, 'could one who has never had a net in his hand and was no longer young learn how to cast it?'

Chellaya was a small round fat man, but he had spoken with great dignity. The fisher knew at once that he was a Brahman and salaamed, touching the ground with his forehead.

'Lord,' he said, 'the boy learns to cast the net when he is still at his mother's breast.'

'O foolish dog of a fisher,' said Chellaya pretending to be very angry, 'can you not understand? Suppose one who was not a fisher and was well on in years wished to fish – for a vow or even for play – could such a one learn to cast the net ?'

The old fisherman screwed up his wrinkled face and looked up at Chellaya doubtfully.

'Lord,' he said, 'I cannot tell. For how could such a thing be? To the fisher his net, as the saying is. Such things are learnt when one is young, as one learns to walk.'

Chellaya looked out over the old man's head to the lagoon. Another fisherman was stealing along in the water ready for the cast. Ah, swish out flew the net. No, nothing – yes, O joy, a gleam of silver in the meshes. Chellaya made up his mind suddenly.

'Now, look here, fellow, – tell me this; could you teach me to cast a net ?'

The old man covered his mouth with his hand, for it is not seemly that a fisher should smile in the presence of a Brahman.

'The lord is laughing at me,' he said respectfully.

'I am not laughing, fellow. I have made a vow to Muniyappa that if he would take away the curse which he laid upon my son's child I would cast a net nightly in the lagoon. Now my son's child is well. Therefore if you will take me tomorrow night to a spot where no one will see us and bring me a net and teach me to cast it, I will give you five measures of rice. And if you speak a word of this to anyone, I will call down upon your head and your child's head ten thousand curses of Muniyappa.'

It is dangerous to risk being cursed by a Brahman, so the fisherman agreed and next evening took Chellaya to a bay in the lagoon and showed him how to cast the net. For an hour Chellaya waded about in the shallow water experiencing a dreadful pleasure. Every moment he glanced over his shoulder to the land to make sure that nobody was in sight; every moment came the pang that he was the first Brahman to pollute his caste by fishing; and every moment came the keen joy of hope that this time the net would swish out and fall in a gentle circle upon a silver fish.

Chellaya caught nothing that night, but he had gone too far to turn back. He gave the fisherman two rupees for the net, and hid it under a rock, and every night he went away to the solitary creek, made a little pile of his white Brahman clothes on the sand, and stepped into the shallow water with his net. There he fished until the sun sank. And sometimes now he caught fish which very reluctantly he had to throw back into the water, for he was afraid to carry them back to his wife.

Very soon a strange rumour began to spread in the town that the Brahman Chellaya had polluted his caste by fishing. At first people would not believe it; such a thing could not happen, for it had never happened before. But at last so many people told the story, – and one man had seen Chellaya carrying a net and another had seen him wading in the lagoon – that everyone began to believe it, the lower castes with great pleasure and the Brahmans with great shame and anger.

Hardly had people begun to believe this rumour than an almost stranger thing began to be talked of. The Brahman Chittampalam, who was Chellaya's neighbour, had polluted his caste, it was said, by carrying earth on his head. And this rumour also was true and it happened in this way.

Chittampalam was a taciturn man and a miser. If his thin scraggy wife used three chillies, where she might have done with two for the curry, he beat her soundly. About the time that Chellaya began to fish in secret, the water in Chittampalam's well began to grow brackish. It became necessary to dig a new well in the compound, but to dig a well means paying a lower caste man to do the work; for the earth that is taken out has to be carried away on the head, and it is pollution for a Brahman to carry earth on his head. So Chittampalam sat in his compound thinking for many days how to avoid paying a man to dig a new well: and meanwhile the taste of the water from the old well became more and more unpleasant. At last it became impossible even for Chittampalam's wife to drink the water; there was only one way out of it; a new well must be dug and he could not bring himself to pay for the digging: he must dig the well himself. So every night for a week Chittampalam went down to the darkest corner of his compound and dug a well and carried earth on his head and thereby polluted his caste.

The other Brahmans were enraged with Chellaya and Chittampalam and, after abusing them and calling them pariahs, they cast them out for ever from the Brahman caste and refused to eat or drink with them or to talk to them; and they took an oath that their children's children should never marry with the grandsons and granddaughters of Chellaya and Chittampalam. But if people of other castes talked to them of the matter, they denied all knowledge of it and swore that no Brahman had ever caught fish or carried earth on his head. Chittampalam was not much concerned at the anger of the Brahmans, for he had saved the hire of a well-digger and he had never taken pleasure in the conversation of other Brahmans and, besides, he shortly after died.

Chellaya, being a small fat man and of a more pleasant and therefore more sensitive nature, felt his sin and the disapproval of his friends deeply. For some days he gave up his fishing, but they were weary days to him and he gained nothing, for the Brahmans still refused to talk to him. All day long in the temple and in his compound he sat and thought of his evenings when he waded in the blue waters of the lagoon, and of the little islands resting like plumes of smoke or feathers upon the sky, and of the line of pink flamingos like thin posts at regular intervals set to mark a channel, and of the silver gleam of darting fish. In the evening, when he knew the fishermen were taking out their nets, his longing became intolerable: he dared not go down to the lagoon for he knew that his desire would master him. So for five nights he sat in his compound. and, as the saying is, his fat went off in desire. On the sixth night he could stand it no longer; once more he polluted his caste by catching fish.

After this Chellaya no longer tried to struggle against himself but continued to fish until at the age of fifty he died. Then, as time went on, the people who had known Chellaya and Chittampalam died too, and the story of how each had polluted his caste began to be forgotten. Only it was known in Yalpanam that no Brahman could marry into those two families, because there was something wrong with their caste. Some said that Chellaya had carried earth on his head and that Chittampalam had caught fish; in any case the descendants of Chellaya and Chittampalam had to go to distant villages to find Brahman wives and husbands for their sons and daughters.

Chellaya's hut and Chittampalam's hut still stand where they stood under the coconut trees by the side of the lagoon, and in one lives Chellaya, the great-great-great-grandson of Chellaya who caught fish, and in the other Chittampalam the great-great-great-grandson of Chittampalam who carried earth on his head. Chittampalam has a very beautiful daughter and Chellaya has one son unmarried. Now this son saw Chittampalam's daughter by accident through the fence of the compound, and he went to his father and said:

'They say that our neighbour's daughter will have a big dowry; should we not make a proposal of marriage?'

The father had often thought of marrying his son to Chittampalam's daughter, not because he had seen her through the compound fence but because he had reason to believe that her dowry would be large. But he had never mentioned it to his wife or to his son, because he knew that it was said that an ancestor of Chittampalam had once dug a well and carried earth on his head. Now however that his son himself suggested the marriage, he approved of the idea, and, as the custom is, told his wife to go to Chittampalam's house and look at the girl. So his wife went formally to Chittampalam's house for the visit preparatory to an offer of marriage, and she came back and reported that the girl was beautiful and fit for even her son to marry.

Chittampalam had himself often thought of proposing to Chellaya that Chellaya's son should marry his daughter, but he had been ashamed to do this because he knew that Chellaya's ancestor had caught fish and thereby polluted his caste. Otherwise the match was desirable, for he would be saved from all the trouble of finding a husband for her in some distant village. However, if Chellaya himself proposed it, he made up his mind not to put any difficulties in the way. The next time that the two met, Chellaya made the proposal and Chittampalam accepted it and then they went back to Chellaya's compound to discuss the question of dowry. As is usual in such cases the father of the girl wants the dowry to be small and the father of the boy wants it to be large, and all sorts of reasons are given on both sides why it should be small or large, and the argument begins to grow warm. The argument became so warm that at last Chittampalam lost his temper and said:

'One thousand rupees! Is that what you want? Why, a fisher should take the girl with no dowry at all!

'Fisher!' shouted Chellaya. 'Who would marry into the pariah caste, that defiles itself by digging wells and carrying earth on its head? You had better give two thousand rupees to a pariah to take your daughter out of your house.'

'Fisher! Low caste dog!' shouted Chittampalam.

'Pariah! screamed Chellaya.

Chittampalam rushed from the compound and for many days the two Brahmans refused to talk a word to one another. At last Chellaya's son, who had again seen the daughter of Chittampalam through the fence of the compound, talked to his father and then to Chittampalam, and the quarrel was healed and they began to discuss again the question of dowry. But the old words rankled and they were still sore, as soon as the discussion began to grow warm it ended once more by their calling each other 'Fisher' and 'Pariah'. The same thing has happened now several times, and Chittampalam is beginning to think of going to distant villages to find a husband for his daughter. Chellaya's son is very unhappy; he goes down every evening and sits by the waters of the blue lagoon on the very spot where his great-great-great-grandfather Chellaya used to sit and watch the fishermen cast their nets.

The Voyage Out

In October 1904, I sailed from Tilbury Docks in the P & O *Syria* for Ceylon. I was a Cadet in the Ceylon Civil Service. To make a complete break with one's former life is a strange, frightening, and exhilarating experience. It has upon one, I think, the effect of a second birth. When one emerges from one's mother's womb one leaves a life of dim security for a world of violent difficulties and dangers. Few, if any, people ever entirely recover from the trauma of being born, and we spend a lifetime unsuccessfully trying to heal the wound, to protect ourselves against the hostility of things and men. But because at birth consciousness is dim and it takes a long time for us to become aware of our envi-ronment, we do not feel a sudden break, and adjustment is slow, lasting indeed a lifetime. I can remember the precise moment of my second birth. The umbilical cord by which I had been attached to my family, to St. Paul's, to Cambridge and Trinity was cut when, leaning over the ship's taffrail, I watched through the dirty, dripping murk and fog of the river my mother and sister waving good-bye and felt the ship begin slowly to move down the Thames to the sea.

To be born again in this way at the age of 24 is a strange expe-rience which imprints a permanent mark upon one's character and one's attitude to life. I was leaving in England everyone and everything I knew; I was going to a place and life in which I really had not the faintest idea of how I should live and what I should be doing. All that I was taking with me from the old life as a contribution to the new and to prepare me for my task of helping to rule the British Empire was 90 large, beautifully printed volumes of Voltaire* and a wire-haired fox-terrier. The first impact of the new life was menacing and depressing. The ship slid down the oily dark waters of the river through cold clammy mist and rain; next day in the Channel it was barely possible to distinguish the cold and gloomy sky from the cold

* The 1784 edition printed in Baskerville type.

and gloomy sea. Within the boat there was the uncomfortable atmosphere of suspicion and reserve which is at first invariably the result when a number of English men and women, strangers to one another, find that they have to live together for a time in a train, a ship, a hotel.

In those days it took, if I remember rightly, three weeks to sail from London to Colombo. By the time we reached Ceylon, we had developed from a fortuitous concourse of isolated human atoms into a complex community with an elaborate system of castes and classes. The initial suspicion and reserve had soon given place to intimate friendships, intrigues, affairs, passionate loves and hates. I learned a great deal from my three weeks on board the P & O *Syria*. Nearly all my fellow-passengers were quite unlike the people whom I had known at home or at Cambridge. On the face of it and of them they were very ordinary persons with whom in my previous life I would have felt that I had little in common except perhaps mutual contempt. I learned two valuable lessons: first how to get on with ordinary persons, and secondly that there are practically no ordinary persons, that beneath the façade of John Smith and Jane Brown there is a strange character and often a passionate individual.

One of the most interesting and unexpected exhibits was Captain L. of the Manchester Regiment, who, with a wife and small daughter, was going out to India. When I first saw and spoke to him, in the arrogant ignorance of youth and Cambridge, I thought he was inevitably the dumb and dummy figure which I imagined to be characteristic of any captain in the Regular Army. Nothing could have been more mistaken. He and his wife and child were in the cabin next to mine, and I became painfully aware that the small girl wetted her bed and that Captain L. and his wife thought that the right way to cure her was to beat her. I had not at that time read *A Child is being Beaten* or any other of the works of Sigmund Freud, but the hysterical shrieks and sobs which came from the next cabin convinced me that beating was not the right way to cure bed-wetting, and my experience with dogs and other animals had taught me that corporal punishment is never a good instrument of education.

Late one night I was sitting in the smoking-room talking to Captain L. and we seemed suddenly to cross the barrier between formality and intimacy. I took my life in my hands and boldly told him that he was wrong to beat his daughter. We sat arguing about this until the lights went out, and next morning to my astonishment he came up to me and told me that I had convinced him and that he would never beat his daughter again. One curious result was that Mrs. L. was enraged with me for interfering and pursued me with bitter hostility until we finally parted for ever at Colombo.

After this episode I saw a great deal of the captain. I found him to be a man of some intelligence and of intense intellectual curiosity, but in his family, his school, and his regiment the speculative mind or conversation was unknown, unthinkable. He was surprised and delighted to find someone who would talk about anything and everything, including God, sceptically. We found a third companion with similar tastes in the Chief Engineer, a dour Scot, who used to join us late at night in the smoking-room with two candles so that we could go on talking and drinking whisky and soda after the lights went out. The captain had another characteristic, shared by me: he had a passion for every kind of game. During the day we played the usual deck games, chess, draughts, and even noughts and crosses, and very late at night when the two candles in the smoking-room began to gutter, he would say to me sometimes: 'And now, Woolf, before the candles go out, we'll play the oldest game in the world,' the oldest game in the world, according to him, being a primitive form of draughts which certain arrangements of stones, in

Greenland and African deserts, show was played all over the world by prehistoric man.

The three weeks which I spent on the P & O *Syria* had a considerable and salutary effect upon me. I found myself able to get along quite well in this new, entirely strange, and rather formidable world into which I had projected myself. I enjoyed adjusting myself to it and to thirty or forty complete strangers. It was fascinating to explore the minds of some and watch the psychological or social antics of others. I became great friends with some and even managed to have a fairly lively flirtation with a young woman which, to my amusement, earned me a long, but very kindly, warning and good advice from one of the middle-aged ladies. The importance of that kind of voyage for a young man with the age and experience or inexperience which were then mine is that the world and society of the boat are a microcosm of the macrocosm in which he will be condemned to spend the rest of his life, and it is probable that his temporary method of adjusting himself to the one will become the permanent method of adjusting to the other. I am sure that it was so to a great extent in my case.

One bitter lesson, comparatively new to me, and an incident which graved it deeply into my mind, are still vivid to me after more than fifty years. I am still, after those fifty years, naively surprised and shocked by the gratuitous inhumanity of so many human beings, their spontaneous malevolence towards one another. There were on the boat three young civil servants, Millington and I going out to Ceylon, and a young man called Scafe who had just passed into the Indian Civil Service. There were also two or three Colombo business men, in particular a large flamboyant Mr. X who was employed in a big Colombo shop. It gradually became clear to us that Mr. X and his friends regarded us with *a priori* malignity because we were civil servants. It was my first experience of the class war and hatred between Europeans which in 1904 were a curious feature of British imperialism in the East.

The British were divided into four well-defined classes: civil servants, army officers, planters, and business men. There was in the last three classes an embryonic feeling against the first. The civil servant was socially in many ways top dog; he was highly paid, exercised considerable and widely distributed power, and with the Sinhalese and Tamils enjoyed much greater prestige than the other classes. The army officers had, of course, high social claims, as they have always and everywhere, but in Ceylon there were too few of them to be of social importance. In Kandy and the mountains, hundreds of British planters lived on their dreary tea estates and they enjoyed superficially complete social equality with the civil servants. They belonged to the same clubs, played tennis together, and occasionally intermarried. But there is no doubt that generally the social position and prospects of a civil servant were counted to be a good deal higher than those of a planter. The attitude of planters' wives with nubile daughters to potential sons-in-law left one in no doubt of this, for the marriage market is an infallible test of social values. The business men were on an altogether lower level. I suppose the higher executives, as they would now be called, the tycoons, if there were any in those days, in Colombo were members of the Colombo Club and moved in the 'highest' society. But all in subordinate posts in banks and commercial firms were socially inferior. In the whole of my seven years in Ceylon I never had a meal with a business man, and when I was stationed in Kandy, every member of the Kandy Club, except one young man, a solicitor, was a civil servant, an army officer, or a planter – they were of course all white men.

White society in India and Ceylon, as you can see in Kipling's stories, was always suburban. In Calcutta and Simla, in Colombo and Nuwara Eliya, the social structure and relations between Europeans rested on the same kind of snobbery, pretentiousness, and false pretensions as they did in Putney or Peckham. No one can understand the aura of life for a young civil servant in Ceylon during the first decade of the twentieth century – or indeed the history of the British Empire – unless he realizes and allows for these facts. It is true that for only one year out of my seven in Ceylon was I personally subjected to the full impact of this social system, because except for my year in Kandy I was in outstations where there were few or no other white people, and there was therefore little or no society. Nevertheless the flavour or climate of one's life was enormously affected, even though one might not always be aware of it, both by this circumambient air of a tropical suburbia and by the complete social exclusion from our social suburbia of all Sinhalese and Tamils.

These facts are relevant to Mr. X's malevolence to me and my two fellow civil servants. None of us, I am sure, gave him the slightest excuse for hating us by putting on airs or side. We were new boys, much too insecure and callow to imagine that we were, as civil servants, superior to business men. Mr. X hated us simply because we were civil servants, and he suffered too, I think, from that inborn lamentable malignity which causes some people to find their pleasure in hurting and humiliating others. Mr. X was always unpleasant to us and one day succeeded during a kind of gymkhana by a piece of violent horseplay in putting Scafe and me in an ignominious position.

It is curious – and then again, if one remembers Freud, it is of course not so curious – that I should remember so vividly, after 56 years, the incident and the hurt and humiliation, the incident being so trivial and so too, on the face of it, the hurt and humiliation. One of the 'turns' in the gymkhana was a pillow-fight between two men sitting on a parallel bar, the one who unseated the other being the winner. Mr. X was organizer and referee.

Scafe and I were drawn against each other in the first round, and when we had got on to the bar and were just preparing for the fray, Mr. X walked up to us and with considerable roughness – we were completely at his mercy – whirled Scafe off the bar in one direction and me in the other. It was, no doubt, a joke, and the spectators, or some of them, laughed.

It was a joke, but then, of course, it was, deep down, particularly for the victims, 'no joke'. Freud with his usual lucidity unravels the nature of this kind of joke in Chapter III, 'The Purposes of Jokes,' of his remarkable book *Jokes and their Relation to the Unconscious*. 'Since our individual childhood, and, similarly, since the childhood of human civilization, hostile impulses against our fellow men have been subject to the same restrictions, the same progressive repression, as our sexual urges.' But the civilized joke against a person allows us to satisfy our hatred of and hostility against him just as the civilized dirty joke allows us to satisfy our repressed sexual urges. Freud continues:

> Since we have been obliged to renounce the expression of hostility by deeds – held back by the passionless third person, in whose interest it is that personal security shall be preserved – we have, just as in the case of sexual aggressiveness, developed a new technique of invective, which aims at enlisting this third person against our enemy. By making our enemy small, inferior, despicable or comic, we achieve in a roundabout way the enjoyment of overcoming him – to which the third person, who has made no efforts, bears witness by his laughter.

Civilization ensured that Mr. X renounced any expression of his innate, malevolent hostility to Scafe and me by undraped physical violence on a respectable P & O liner, but under the drapery of a joke he was able to make us 'small, inferior, despicable, and comic' and so satisfy his malevolence and enjoy our humiliation to which the laughter of the audience bore witness. Even when I am not the object of it, I have always felt this kind of spontaneous malignity, this pleasure in the gratuitous causing of pain, to be profoundly depressing. I still remember Mr. X, though we never spoke to each other on board ship and I never saw him again after we disembarked at Colombo.

The Pearl Fishery

On January 28th I received a telegram from the G.A. Jaffna asking me whether I was well enough to take up in the middle of February a special appointment as Koddu Superintendent at the Pearl Fishery. It was obviously an extremely interesting job, so I wired back 'Yes,' and next day set out to Jaffna.

The Ceylon Pearl Fishery is said to go back to very ancient times. The pearl oyster (Pinctada), which is more nearly related to the mussel than to the edible oyster, breeds on the pearl banks in the Gulf of Mannar some miles off the barren uninhabited coast of the Mannar District in the Northern Province. The oysters breed and produce pearls very erratically. In my day there was a Superintendent of Pearl Fisheries, Hornell, who had a steamer at his disposal and, I think, a dredger. He inspected the oyster banks in the autumn and if he found that there were sufficient mature oysters and the average number of pearls in the samples dredged up was satisfactory, the Government proclaimed a Pearl Fishery for the following February. As the Fishery was in the Northern Province waters, the G.A. Jaffna was in complete charge of it and had to make all the arrangements for it. He took with him four or five white officers. In 1906 he had three civil servants, John Scott, the A.G.A. Mannar, and two specially seconded, i.e. Malcolm Stevenson (three years my senior) and myself, and an Assistant Superintendent of Police.

The Pearl Fishery camp was always at Marichchukaddi, which as the crow flies is about 80 miles from Jaffna. When there is no Fishery, Marichchukaddi is merely a name on a map, a stretch of sandy scrub jungle with the thick jungle beginning half a mile or so inland. There was no road to it, only a rough sandy track along the coast to Mannar, so that the only way to reach it was by sea. There was no harbour and all the bigger boats and steamers from India and Colombo had to lie anchored offshore. About twenty to thirty thousand people came from all over Asia to the Fishery, divers, jewellers, dealers, merchants, traders, financiers, shopkeepers, dacoits, criminals. To house these people the Government, i.e. the G.A., built a large town on the desert of sand, containing bungalows for himself and the other Government officers, huts for the divers, traders, and boutique keepers, a court, police station, prison, and hospital. All these buildings were of timber with cadjan roofs. This temporary town was laid out in regular streets: Main Street, Tank Street, New Street, New Moor Street.

It was, I think, on February 15th that I sailed from Jaffna to Marichchukaddi in an open native boat. It took me a day and a half to reach Marichchukaddi. I lay on a mattress with the sun beating down upon me during the day and the immense canopy of stars seemingly just above my head at night. We had to sail first south-west round Mannar and through the little islands of Adam's Bridge and then south to the Fishery. There is – or was – to me always something extraordinarily romantic in this kind of setting off entirely alone in a small boat into the unknown. The wind would fall and we lay becalmed in an immense silence and then the breeze would again steal up across the water and we would begin once more to go gently through the sea. It really was as though time stood still. One's life, one's universe had been reduced to the bare sea and the bare sky, day and night, sun and stars. Whether or when one was to arrive lost all importance; the complete solitude away from any trace of civilization or taint of civilized people, with its gentle, soothing melancholy, seemed, as it always does, to purge the passions. When they ran my boat up on to the sandy beach at Marichchukaddi and I jumped down into the sand, I felt that, though my body was unwashed and unshaved, my mind had been curiously cleaned and purified. Naturally I was instantly and appropriately re-called to reality. The G.A.'s bungalow had been built on a small hillock of sand overlooking the beach and I walked up the slope to report my arrival and find out where my bungalow would be.

When I reached the top, there was Mrs. Lewis sitting outside the bungalow with a table by her side and a gramophone on the table blaring into the evening sky above and the sand and sea below 'Funiculi, funicula'. 'Hallo! Hallo! Mr. Woolf. I'm glad to see you,' the jolly female voice was louder even than the Neapolitan singers. 'How are you? Come on, come on and have a drink and listen to my new record.' I was back once more in civilization.

It was certainly a very primitive form of civilization, apart from Mrs. Lewis and her gramophone. The methods on which we ran the Fishery seemed to me antediluvian, primordial. The fishing was actually done by Arab or Tamil divers. There were 4,090 Arabs who came down from the Persian Gulf in dhows. The dhows were commanded by chiefs or sheiks, some of whom, I think, commanded several dhows. There were 4,577 Tamil and Moor divers, most of whom came from India; they fished from open native boats. The Fishery lasted from February 20th to April 3rd. Every morning about 2 or 3 a.m., if the wind and sea were favourable, the Superintendent fired a gun which was the signal that the dhows and boats might be launched and sail off to the Pearl Banks. The method of fishing was this: each diver (if he was an Arab, using a bone nose-clip) stood on a large flat stone through which ran a rope held by a man in the boat, called a man-duck. At a signal from the diver the man paid out the rope as fast as he could and the diver on the stone was carried to the floor of the sea. There he shovelled oysters into a large basket which was attached to another rope. When he shook the rope, he was hauled up by his man-duck into the boat. This went on all day. There were 473 boats divided into two fleets which fished on alternate days; the largest number of boats to go out on anyone day was 286. In the afternoon the Superintendent fired a gun out on the Banks and all the dhows and boats raced for the shore.*

* Some of the boats were towed in by a Government steamer.

The Arabs ran their boats up on to the sand and with a tremendous shouting rushed into the koddu carrying their oysters in great baskets. The koddu was an enormous fenced square enclosure with nine open huts running down it from end to end. Each hut was divided into compartments, and each boat as soon as it arrived had to bring in its load of oysters and deposit it in a compartment dividing it up into three equal heaps. The Koddu Superintendent, of whom I was one, then went round and chose two out of the three heaps as the Government's share, leaving the other heap to be gathered up by the divers and to be taken with a roar of shouting out of the koddu.

Later in the evening the Government's oysters were auctioned by the G.A. When the first divers rushed their shares out of the koddu, they were surrounded by a crowd of pearl dealers and merchants who bid against one another for the oysters. Those who succeeded in getting some, hurried away and opened the oysters to see whether the number and quality of the pearls which they contained were above or below average. What they found in these samples determined the bidding at the Government auction in the evening. The method of extracting the pearls from the oysters was primitive and insanitary. The oysters were put into a canoe or dug-out and allowed to rot for several days; when the oysters had decayed, seawater was put into the canoe which was gently rocked and the seawater gradually poured off; there upon the bottom of the canoe was a sediment of sand, putrid oyster, and pearls. As the Fishery went on and the whole camp became full of thousands of putrid and putrescent oysters, a horrible smell hung over it and us night and day and myriads of flies swarmed over everything. Every particle of food had to be kept closely covered until the last moment before you popped it into your mouth.

John Scott, as A.G.A., was responsible for law and order in the camp, sat as Police Magistrate, and was Koddu Superintendent; I was Assistant Koddu Superintendent; Stevenson was Superintendent of Police. Stevenson and I shared a bungalow. I was also Additional Police Magistrate, and when I had time helped with the supervision of the camp. The work of the Koddu Superintendents was onerous and exhausting. In theory the fishing ended each day in the early afternoon, the dhows raced back before the wind blowing from the sea, the divers dumped their oysters and the Government had taken its share and the koddu was cleared by the late afternoon. This ideal timetable rarely worked out in practice. For the dhows to get back to the shore from the Banks reasonably early in the afternoon, they required a fairly brisk south-west wind. Very often they got a light or contrary wind or no wind at all, and they had to tack or even row. When this happened, the boats would drop in one by one all night long and even on into the following day.

At one time we were fishing a Bank nearly 20 miles away and the boats, with a favourable wind, took four or five hours to get in, but the wind was consistently unfavourable and day after day they took 12, 24, or even 36 hours to reach the shore. A Koddu Superintendent had to be in the koddu the whole time, keeping order among the hundreds of shouting, gesticulating Arabs in the light of flickering oil lamps and torches and taking over the Government's oysters. In the day one trudged up and down the koddu through the sand under a blazing sky. 'It is like walking about hour after hour,' I wrote in a letter, 'in a hell twice as mad as the coaling at Port Said. It is merely coolie work supervising this and the counting and issuing of about one or two million oysters a day, for the Arabs will do anything if you hit them hard enough with a walking stick, an occupation in which I have been engaged for the most part of the last

3 days and nights.' The heat and the flies made everyone feel ill and at the most hectic moment Stevenson went down with malaria and Scott was also ill. I was almost continually in the koddu night and day and, when not there, patrolling the camp or trying police court cases. In a letter to Lytton I wrote: 'The work is consequently going on day and night and I have only been about 3 or 4 hours in bed out of the last 72.'

I think that my recovery from typhoid had given me a new lease of life and, as I often said at the time, a new inside. I know I felt extraordinarily well and completely untirable. But I also experienced in the sands of Marichchukaddi one of those sudden, instantaneous cures which at the moment seem a divine miracle and exhilarate one so that for a time one becomes immune to all the ills of the flesh. When I left Jaffna, I was suffering from an eczema which is very usual in Ceylon. But the heat and continual walking in the sand of the koddu made it infinitely worse and my thighs and scrotum were covered and inflamed with an intolerable rash. The pain and discomfort of walking about for five or six hours on end in the sun in this condition were appalling. I bore it for three or four days and then, after I left the koddu one morning, I went to the Medical Officer and asked him whether he could do anything. He gave me a lotion which I immediately put on. The result was, as I said, literally to me a miracle. When I put the lotion on I was in a raw and bleeding state, and I had to go back to the koddu in the afternoon. By that time, I was more or less comfortable – and I had been in acute discomfort for days – and when I left the koddu about midnight, I was recovered.

There was a great deal to be said against our rule of. Ceylon, which, of course, was bleak 'imperialism' or what is now fashionably called colonialism. One of the good things about it, however, was the extraordinary absence of the use of force in everyday life and government. Ceylon in 1906 was the exact opposite of a 'police state'. There were very few police and outside Colombo and Kandy not a single soldier. From the point of view of law and order nothing could have been more dangerously precarious than the Pearl Fishery camp, a temporary town of 30,000 or 40,000 men, many of whom were habitual criminals. As the Fishery went on, the town became fuller and fuller of a highly valuable form of property, pearls. There was one danger which was a perpetual nightmare to us and which I will deal with later, but apart from that we four civil servants never even thought about the possibility of our not being able to maintain law and order. And we were quite right. In the koddu we had an interpreter, some police constables, and a few Tamils whose duty it was to take over the Government's shares of the oysters and see that no one touched them. Otherwise I was single-handed and had to keep order among a thousand or more Arabs pouring into an enclosed space dimly lit, carrying heavy sacks and baskets of oysters, and all desperately anxious to find a good empty compartment and to get out of the koddu as quickly as possible with their share of oysters. At the time it seemed to me quite easy and natural to do this with a loud voice and a walking stick, though I was by nature, as I have already said more than once, a nervous and cowardly person.

The Arabs fascinated me, both in themselves and because of the contrast between them and the Tamils. The Tamil crowd was low in tone, rather timid, depressed and complaining in adversity. The Arab superficially was the exact opposite. At the end of the Fishery I went in a small steamer, packed with about 1,000 Arabs and Tamils, to Paumben in India. The men swarmed everywhere over all the decks and overflowed into the three small cabins and into the box of a saloon. The sea was rough all night and they were seasick most of the time. In a letter to Lytton describing this I contrasted the behaviour of the Semitic with that of the Dravidian, perhaps somewhat unfairly.

The Tamils, I wrote, were 'huddling together, squabbling and complaining, but the Arab is superb, he has the grand manner, absolutely saturnine, no fuss or excitement, but one could see when day broke that every Arab had room and to spare to stretch full length in his blanket on the deck.'

The Arabs were not always calm; when they rushed up the beach with their great sacks of oysters, talking at the top of their voices, shouting, laughing, the noise was tremendous, and it was wonderful when above the tumult one heard a voice from the sea crying trailingly and melodiously 'Ab-d-ul-la! Ab-d-ul-la!' The men of each boat always kept closely together, and among the Arabs were a certain number of negroes, said to have been or even to be slaves. Every Arab seemed to have his own copper coffeepot. In one boat there was a gigantic negro – he must have been six foot five inches or six foot six inches – he was wrapped about with several sacks, and, tied together with a rope, dangling and clattering on his back were always 15 or 20 copper coffeepots which he carried for his companions. One of the ways in which the Arab was different from the Tamil was the way in which he treated the white man in authority. The Tamil treated one as someone apart; he would never dream of touching one, for instance. The Arabs, on the other hand, although extremely polite, treated me as a fellow human being. If anything went wrong or there was a dispute which I had to settle, they would surround me and make long eloquent guttural speeches, and often if one of them got excited, he would put his hand on my shoulder to emphasize the torrent of his words. Once towards the end of the Fishery, when they all knew me well and I had got to know some of them quite well, one of them before he left the koddu rushed up to me, put one hand on my shoulder, made a short speech, and then took off his camelhair head-dress and the nose-clip which hung round his neck and gave them to me.

It was this attitude of human equality which accounted for the fact, oddly enough, that I hit them with a walking stick, whereas in the whole of my time in Ceylon I never struck, or would have dared to strike, a Tamil or a Sinhalese. When all the boats were coming in together, the koddu became a struggling mass of packed human beings, Arabs hauling in their sacks of oysters from the beach or carrying them out to sell at the other end. To get through the crowd from compartment to compartment in order to see that the division of the oysters was properly made – as I had to do – I simply had to fight my way through, shouting 'Get out of the way – get out of the way,' and the Arabs were vastly amused when I used my walking stick to clear a passage through them.

One scene in the koddu, connected with the Arabs, of a very different kind, tragic and beautiful, I shall never forget. I had been in the koddu all night and the last Arabs and the last oysters were leaving in the early hours of the morning. I was just going to leave myself when an Arab came in from the beach and told me that one of his men had died when diving out on the banks and that the body and the rest of his crew were still on board. As smallpox had broken out in the camp, I kept all the Arabs on board and sent for the Medical Officer. When he came, I went down to the shore with him. Four men waded out to the boat: the corpse was lifted out and placed on their shoulders. Forty years ago, when the scene was still vividly in my memory, I wrote down a description of it, and I think it is better to quote it here verbatim rather than to write it afresh allover again. The four men 'waded back slowly; the feet of the dead man stuck out, toes pointing up, very stark over the shoulders of the men in front. The body was laid on the sand. The bearded face of the dead man looked very calm, very dignified in the faint light.' The doctor made his examination, and when at last he said it was not smallpox, I told the sheik in charge of the boat that he could remove the body. An Arab, the brother of the dead man, was sitting on the sand near his head. 'He covered himself with sackcloth. I heard him weeping. It was very silent, very cold and still on the shore in the early dawn. A tall figure stepped forward, it was the Arab sheik, the leader of the boat. He laid his hand on the head of the weeping man and spoke to him calmly, eloquently, compassionately. I didn't understand Arabic, but I could understand what he was saying. The dead man had lived, had worked, had died. He had died working, without suffering, as men should desire to die. He had left a son behind him. The speech went on calmly, eloquently, I heard continually the word Khallas – all is finished. I watched the figures outlined against the grey sky – the long lean outline of the corpse with the toes sticking up so straight and stark, the crouching huddled figure of the weeping man, and the tall upright sheik standing by his side. They were motionless, sombre, mysterious, part of the grey sea, of the grey sky.

'Suddenly the dawn broke red in the sky. The sheik stopped, motioned silently to the four men. They lifted the dead man on to their shoulders. They moved away down the shore by the side of the sea which began to stir under the cold wind. By their side walked the sheik, his hand laid gently on the brother's arm. I watched them move away, silent, dignified. And over the shoulders of the men I saw the feet of the dead man with the toes sticking up straight and stark.'

There was so much work and so much illness during the two months of the Fishery that we had very little time for social life. It was rare for us all to be free of an evening for dinner and bridge and 'Funiculi, funicula,' which was what Mrs. Lewis pined for. This was no doubt a pity for we all got on very well together. Scott, the A.G.A., who had been a scholar of King's, I had known for some time and liked. Stevenson was an amusing

Irishman and talked incessantly like an Irishman in a novel; he was also extremely able and became Sir Malcolm Stevenson, K.C.M.G., Governor of Cyprus. A curious incident happened to us one night. We had been dining with the G.A. and were walking back to our bungalow. The night was very dark and we had a boy with us lighting our way over the sand with a dim hurricane lamp. Stevenson was discoursing to me and at one point stopped characteristically and faced me so that the fountain of words should be as little impeded as possible. We stood facing each other a few feet apart and, as he talked he slowly twirled round and round, a few inches in front of my nose and of his, a walking stick. Suddenly the stick caught on something on the ground and whizzed it up in the air between us. As it fell back on the ground, Stevenson brought his stick down on it. The boy rushed up with the hurricane lamp and there upon the ground by our feet was a tic polonga, a Russell's viper, one of the deadliest of Ceylon snakes.

I always liked the job of patrolling the camp late at night. One or other of us invariably did this to see that the police were on their beats and awake and that nothing suspicious was going on. The danger which perpetually hung over our heads was that some gang of malefactors would set fire to the camp and then, in the panic which followed, start looting. This had been tried more than once and had in fact a year or two before succeeded. In a fresh wind the wood and cadjan huts went up in flames like tinder and on that occasion nearly the whole camp was destroyed in an hour or two. When one patrolled, however late it was, there were always people walking about or sitting in front of their huts. Very often a pearl dealer or merchant would invite one to sit down with him and have a small cup of Turkish coffee. As the Fishery went on and they got to know me, they would show me some of the pearls they had got from purchased oysters or bought from other people.

Once I saw an almost naked coolie walking round the dealers' quarter, clutching something tightly in his hand. I guessed it to be a pearl and asked him to let me see it. He opened his hand for a second, just long enough for me to see one of the largest and most perfect pearls I saw during the Fishery.

Notes

1. A shortened game of billiards, where the first to score 100 points wins.
2. Delirium tremens.
3. An agent or representative, especially one of political importance.

Biographical note

Leonard Sidney Woolf was born in London in 1880, the third of ten children. He was educated at St Paul's School, London, and won a scholarship to study classics at Trinity College, Cambridge; it was here that he met Lytton Strachey, Clive Bell, John Maynard Keynes and E.M. Forster, who were to form the core of what was later to be known as the Bloomsbury group.

In 1904 Woolf joined the Ceylon Civil Service, and was stationed at Jaffna. Four years later he was made assistant government agent in the Southern Province of Ceylon, where he administered the District of Hambantota. These years were to shape him both artistically and politically.

He returned to the United Kingdom in 1911 for a year's leave, but resigned in 1912 and married Virginia Stephen the same year. As a couple, Leonard and Virginia were influential in the Bloomsbury group.

Woolf's first novel, *The Village and the Jungle*, was published in 1913. Together with Virginia he bought a hand-operated printing press and founded the Hogarth Press in 1917, originally as a hobby: their first publication was a pamphlet of two stories, one by Leonard, one by Virginia. Named after their house in Richmond, it became an established publishing house following the success of Virginia's *Kew Gardens* in 1919, and was home to works by Katherine Mansfield, T.S. Eliot, Clive Bell, Robert Graves, E.M. Forster and Vita Sackville-West, amongst others.

Woolf contributed to and edited various journals, wrote numerous sociological and political works, and continued as director of the Hogarth Press until his death in 1969.

HESPERUS PRESS

Hesperus Press, as suggested by the Latin motto, is committed to bringing near what is far – far both in space and time. Works written by the greatest authors, and unjustly neglected or simply little known in the English-speaking world, are made accessible through new translations and a completely fresh editorial approach. Through these classic works, the reader is introduced to the greatest writers from all times and all cultures.

For more information on Hesperus Press, please visit our website: **www.hesperuspress.com**

ET REMOTISSIMA PROPE

MODERN VOICES

SELECTED TITLES FROM HESPERUS PRESS

Author	Title	Foreword writer
Mikhail Bulgakov	*A Dog's Heart*	A.S. Byatt
Mikhail Bulgakov	*The Fatal Eggs*	Doris Lessing
Anthony Burgess	*The Eve of St Venus*	
Colette	*Claudine's House*	Doris Lessing
Marie Ferranti	*The Princess of Mantua*	
Beppe Fenoglio	*A Private Affair*	
F. Scott Fitzgerald	*The Popular Girl*	Helen Dunmore
F. Scott Fitzgerald	*The Rich Boy*	John Updike
Graham Greene	*No Man's Land*	David Lodge
Franz Kafka	*Metamorphosis*	Martin Jarvis
Franz Kafka	*The Trial*	Zadie Smith
D.H. Lawrence	*Wintry Peacock*	Amit Chaudhuri
Rosamond Lehmann	*The Gipsy's Baby*	Niall Griffiths
Carlo Levi	*Words are Stones*	Anita Desai
André Malraux	*The Way of the Kings*	Rachel Seiffert
Katherine Mansfield	*In a German Pension*	Linda Grant
Katherine Mansfield	*Prelude*	William Boyd
Vladimir Mayakovsky	*My Discovery of America*	Colum McCann
Luigi Pirandello	*Loveless Love*	
Françoise Sagan	*The Unmade Bed*	
Jean-Paul Sartre	*The Wall*	Justin Cartwright
Bernard Shaw	*The Adventures of the Black Girl in Her Search for God*	Colm Tóibín
Georges Simenon	*Three Crimes*	